Geronimo Stilton
ENGLISH!

7 LET'S GO TO THE BEACH! 到沙灘去！

U0061310

新雅文化事業有限公司
www.sunya.com.hk

Geronimo Stilton English
LET'S GO TO THE BEACH! 到沙灘去！

作　　者：Geronimo Stilton 謝利連摩·史提頓
譯　　者：申倩
責任編輯：王燕參
封面繪圖：Giuseppe Facciotto
插圖繪畫：Claudio Cernuschi, Andrea Denegri, Daria Cerchi
內文設計：Angela Ficarelli, Raffaella Picozzi
出　　版：新雅文化事業有限公司
　　　　　香港筲箕灣耀興道3號東匯廣場9樓
　　　　　營銷部電話：（852）2562 0161
　　　　　客戶服務部電話：（852）2976 6559
　　　　　傳真：（852）2597 4003
　　　　　網址：http://www.sunya.com.hk
　　　　　電郵：marketing@sunya.com.hk
發　　行：香港聯合書刊物流有限公司
　　　　　香港新界大埔汀麗路36號中華商務印刷大廈3字樓
　　　　　電話：（852）2150 2100　傳真：（852）2407 3062
　　　　　電郵：info@suplogistics.com.hk
印　　刷：C & C Offset Printing Co.,Ltd
　　　　　香港新界大埔汀麗路36號
版　　次：二〇一一年二月初版
　　　　　10 9 8 7 6 5 4 3 2 1

CONTENTS
目錄

BENJAMIN'S CLASSMATES
班哲文的老師和同學們

Maestra Topitilla
托比蒂拉・德・托比莉斯

Rarin
拉琳

Diego
迪哥

Rupa
露芭

Tui
杜爾

David
大衞

Sakura
櫻花

Mohamed
穆哈麥德

Tian Kai
田凱

Oliver
奧利佛

Milenko
米蘭哥

Trippo
特里普

Carmen
卡敏

Atina
阿提娜

Esmeralda
愛絲梅拉達

Pandora
潘朵拉

Takeshi
北野

Kuti
菊花

Benjamin
班哲文

Hsing
阿星

Laura
羅拉

Kiku
奇哥

Antonia
安東妮婭

Liza
麗莎

GERONIMO AND HIS FRIENDS

謝利連摩和他的家鼠朋友們

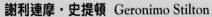

謝利連摩・史提頓 Geronimo Stilton
一個古怪的傢伙,簡直可以說是一隻笨拙的文化鼠。他是《鼠民公報》的總裁,正花盡心思改變報紙業的歷史。

菲・史提頓 Tea Stilton
謝利連摩的妹妹,她是《鼠民公報》的特派記者,同時也是一個運動愛好者。

班哲文・史提頓 Benjamin Stilton
謝利連摩的小侄兒,常被叔叔稱作「我的小乳酪」,是一隻感情豐富的小老鼠。

潘朵拉・華之鼠 Pandora Woz
柏蒂・活力鼠的小侄女、班哲文最好的朋友,是一隻活潑開朗的小老鼠。

柏蒂・活力鼠 Patty Spring
美麗迷人的電視新聞工作者,致力於她熱愛的電視事業。

賴皮 Trappola
謝利連摩的表弟,非常喜歡食物,風趣幽默,是一隻饞嘴、愛開玩笑的老鼠,善於將歡樂傳遞給每一隻鼠。

麗萍姑媽 Zia Lippa
謝利連摩的姑媽,對鼠十分友善,又和藹可親,只想將最好的給身邊的鼠。

艾拿 Iena
謝利連摩的好朋友,充滿活力,熱愛各項運動,他希望能把對運動的熱誠傳給謝利連摩。

史奎克・愛管閒事鼠 Ficcanaso Squitt
謝利連摩的好朋友,是一個非常有頭腦的私家偵探,總是穿着一件黃色的乾濕褸。

TOPAZIA BEACH
妙鼠城沙灘

親愛的小朋友，你喜歡去沙灘嗎？我以一千塊莫澤雷勒乳酪發誓，我是非常非常喜歡去沙灘的！但是我卻不大喜歡乘船！為什麼？答案簡單極了，因為……我會暈船！今天我決定帶班哲文、潘朵拉和我的女朋友……就是柏蒂啦，一起去沙灘玩！請你也帶着小水桶和游泳圈跟我們一起去吧，今天我們要在沙灘學英語呢！

I have got my bathing suit, my suntan lotion, my sunglasses...

跟我謝利連摩·史提頓一起學英文，
就像玩遊戲一樣簡單好玩！

你可以一邊看着圖畫一邊讀。
以下有幾個標誌，你要特別留意：

當看到 🔵 標誌時，你可以聽CD，
一邊聽，一邊跟着朗讀，還可以跟
着一起唱歌。

當看到 ✪ 標誌時，你可以和朋友
們一起玩遊戲，或者嘗試回答問
題。題目很簡單，它們對鞏固你所
學過的內容很有幫助。

當看到 ❗ 標誌時，你要注意看一
下格子裏的生字，反覆唸幾遍，掌
握發音。

最後，不要忘記完成小測驗和練習
冊裏的問題！看看你有多聰明吧。

祝大家學得開開心心！

謝利連摩·史提頓

7

ON THE BEACH 在沙灘上

班哲文和潘朵拉想堆一座很特別很特別的沙堡壘。雖然他們胸有成竹，不過還是需要柏蒂阿姨的幫忙。我以一千塊莫澤雷勒乳酪發誓，這真是太好玩了！沙灘上還有很多有趣的東西，你知道這些東西用英語該怎麼說嗎？一起來學習吧！

changing room

shower

sunglasses

sea

beac

life ring

lifeguard

sunhat

beach towel

sand

sandcastle

bucket

seashell

rubber ring

sand moulds

spade

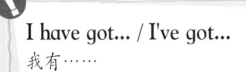

I have got... / I've got...
我有……

I've got a red bucket.

I've got a yellow bucket.

Pandora and Benjamin are making a sandcastle.

beach umbrella

deckchair

flip-flops

suntan lotion

sandals

bathing suit / swimsuit

crab

sunbed

I've got a green marble.

I've got a blue marble.

I've got a yellow marble.

Benjamin, Pandora and Geronimo are playing marbles on a sand track.

LET'S GO SWIMMING!

我在沙灘上感到熱極了，很想下水降降溫，但又害怕自己被太陽曬得頭暈暈的，會忘記怎麼游泳……幸好艾拿走過來帶我一起下水。艾拿真有辦法，我不再怕水了！

班哲文和潘朵拉一邊游泳，還一邊學習用英語說出一些有關游泳的詞彙，你也來一起學習吧！

! **Have you got...?**
你有……嗎？/ 你們有……嗎？
I haven't got...
我沒有……

⭐ 試着用英語說出下面的句子：

(a) 我們有一張浮牀。

(b) 班哲文和潘朵拉有一隻橡皮艇。

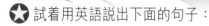

答案：
a) We have got an inflatable mattress.
b) Benjamin and Pandora have got a rubber dinghy.

一起去游泳！

flippers 　蛙鞋
inflatable mattress 　浮牀
rubber dinghy 　橡皮艇
rubber ring 　游泳圈
snorkel 　潛水換氣裝置
underwater mask 　潛水面罩
beach towel 　沙灘毛巾
get dry 　抹乾

AT THE HARBOUR 在碼頭

泡過清涼的海水後，艾拿邀請我們乘帆船出海去。班哲文和潘朵拉興奮極了，但會暈船的我卻不打算跟着去，我推說自己在碼頭散散步就行了。我在碼頭看到很多東西，請你跟着我一起用英語說出來吧！

ship

rock

port / harbour

lighthouse

fishing boat

boat

rowing boat

oar

This rowing boat has got two oars.

fisherman

harbour office

fishing net

sailor

Fishermen have got fishing nets.

12

Let's Go to the Seaside!

Let's go to the seaside!
I have got my bathing suit,
my suntan lotion, my sunglasses,
I've got my flippers
and my underwater mask.
Let's dive in, let's dive in... into the sea!
Let's go to the seaside!

sailing boat

sail

ferry

TOP 1

motorboat

rubber dinghy

fish

life jacket

That sailing boat has got white sails.

13

THE SAILING BOAT 帆船

可是，艾拿卻堅持要所有鼠都看看他的帆船。最先登船的是班哲文和潘朵拉，柏蒂最後說服了我上船，還牽着我的手爪一起登船，那麼現在……我以一千塊莫澤雷勒乳酪發誓，我們都在船上了。我們在船上看到了各種各樣的設施，一起用英語說說看。

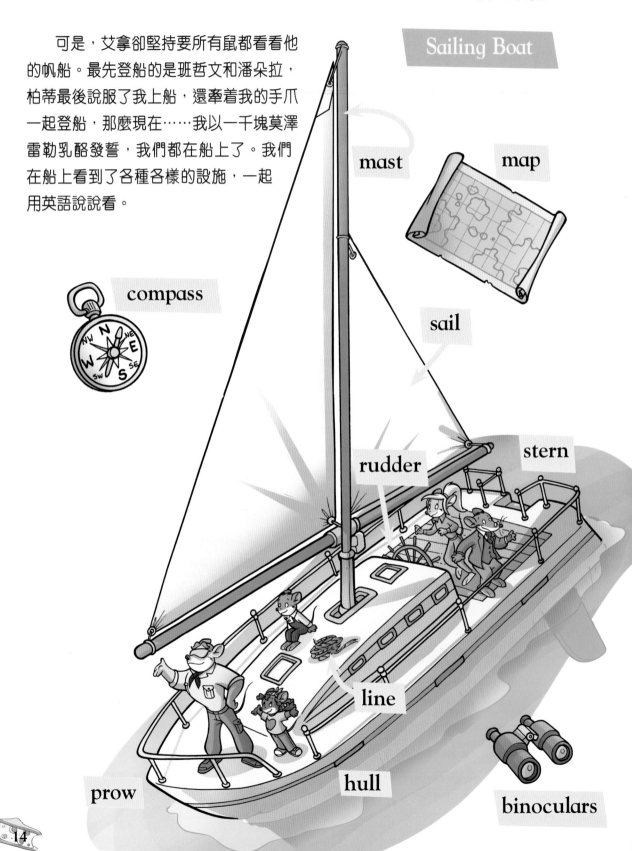

Sailing Boat

mast

map

compass

sail

rudder

stern

line

prow

hull

binoculars

his 他的
her 她的

He has got his map.

She has got her binoculars.

He has got his compass.

He has got shivers.

⭐ 1. 試着用英語説出下列詞彙：小船、手划船、漁船、渡輪、地圖、指南針、雙筒望遠鏡。

⭐ 2. 艾拿、潘朵拉、班哲文分別拿着什麼？請用英語説出來。

2. Lena has got his map. Pandora has got her binoculars. Benjamin has got his compass.
1. boat, rowing boat, fishing boat, ferry, map, compass, binoculars.

答案：

15

HOORAY FOR DOLPHINS!
海豚萬歲！

　　乘帆船出海真是太好玩了，還能看到海豚呢！班哲文和潘朵拉希望學習各種海洋生物的英文名稱，所以柏蒂就拿出一張漂亮的海洋生物大海報，逐一教他們怎樣用英語說出各種海洋生物的名稱，你也來一起學習吧！

Underwater we can see...

I'm afraid of sharks.

starfish

sea urchin

seahorse

coral

sponge

sea anemone

seaweed

jellyfish

tuna

octopus

swordfish

shark

dolphin

sole

be afraid of
害怕

salmon

bass

anchovy

sardine

16

A starfish has got five arms.

An octopus has got eight tentacles.

Dolphins have got a dorsal fin.

Seashells have different shapes and colours.

SUNSET ON THE SEA
在海邊看日落

今天真是奇妙的一天！大家都玩得很開心，當然啦，我很多時候都會臉色發青……因為我暈船暈得很厲害！太好了！終於回到了碼頭，剛好遇上日落，於是我邀請柏蒂一起在海邊浪漫散步……

The sun is setting, the sky is changing colour.

When we were sailing, the wind was blowing, the sea was rough.

sky

sun

reflection on the water

The sun has set. It's evening, night is coming.

Now the wind has dropped, the sea is calm and smooth.

The wind was blowing.
風正在吹着。

It's very beautiful, isn't it?

Yes, the sunset is always beautiful.

A SONG FOR YOU!

Track 2

We Go Sailing

The boat goes
on the waves,
the dolphins
are around me
and the sun is setting
while the wind is blowing.

〈消失的沙〉

安妮馬翠斯：歡迎來到妙鼠城的沙灘！堆沙比賽快要開始了！

麗萍姑媽：班哲文，你準備好了嗎？

班哲文：準備好了，麗萍姑婆。

潘朵拉：但是……你聞到……一陣腐爛的巴馬乳酪的味道嗎？

安妮馬翠斯：預備，去！比賽開始了！

班哲文：這氣味真難聞！究竟是從哪裏傳來的？

潘朵拉：小心呀，班哲文！你把沙弄到了我的……

潘朵拉：但是……嚼嚼嚼……這味道……

潘朵拉：這不是……沙，這是腐爛的巴馬乳酪。

史柏力叔叔：她說得對！

安妮馬翠斯：比賽暫停！

麗萍姑媽：這裏根本沒有沙，就算你挖兩米深，也不會有沙的。

謝利連摩：我們一定要調查清楚這宗神秘事件。

在妙鼠城的碼頭……
班哲文：史柏力叔叔，你是大海的專家……
史柏力叔叔：……我當然會幫忙啦！

史柏力叔叔：昨天晚上，一艘紅色的郵輪停靠在碼頭……它也散發出這種氣味。

史柏力叔叔：看！那艘郵輪在那裏，它正駛離這裏。
班哲文：叔叔，我們坐快艇去追它吧！

謝利連摩：噢！快艇？

於是，當他們接近那艘郵輪的時候……
史柏力叔叔：船上的人快出來！你們已經被包圍了！

謝利連摩：快點！我感到很不舒服。我想回到岸上去！

船員甲：我們投降了！
船員乙：我們從你們的沙灘偷了這些沙。

潘朵拉：你們為什麼要偷沙？你們想把這些沙運去哪裏？

船員甲：我們有幾噸已過期的巴馬乳酪要棄掉⋯⋯
船員乙：⋯⋯而我們沙灘上的沙被污染了，所以想用妙鼠城那美麗的沙代替。

因此，當所有的沙回到妙鼠城的沙灘後⋯⋯
安妮馬翠斯：今年堆沙比賽的冠軍得主是班哲文和潘朵拉。大家都為你們的精彩作品鼓掌祝賀。

The End

班哲文：這也要歸功於史柏力叔叔！
史柏力叔叔：我很感動啊！
麗萍姑媽：我為你感到驕傲！

TEST 小測驗

⭐ 1. 看看下面的圖畫，用英語説出以下的詞彙。

(a)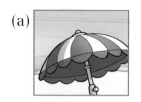
沙灘傘

(b)
游泳圈

(c)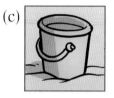
水桶

(d)
防曬油

(e)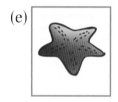
海星

(f)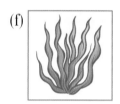
海草

(g)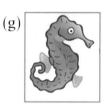
海馬

(h)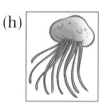
水母

⭐ 2. 用英語説出以下的詞彙。

(a) 魚	(b) 漁夫	(c) 漁網	(d) 漁船
(e) 快艇	(f) 碼頭	(g) 帆	(h) 燈塔

⭐ 3. 以「I've got...」作開頭，用英語説出以下的句子。

(a) 我有一個藍色的水桶。　　(b) 我有一個紅色的水桶。

(c) 我有一艘快艇。　　(d) 我有一個潛水面罩。

⭐ 4. 以「I haven't got...」作開頭，用英語説出以下的句子。

(a) 我沒有浮牀。　　(b) 我沒有沙灘毛巾。

(c) 我沒有小船。　　(d) 我沒有帆船。

DICTIONARY 詞典

（英、粵、普發聲）

A

anchovy　鯷魚

ashore　岸上

B

bass　鱸魚

bathing suit

　　泳衣（普：游泳衣）

beach　沙灘

beach towel　沙灘毛巾

beach umbrella　沙灘傘

beautiful　美麗

binoculars　雙筒望遠鏡

boat　小船

bucket　水桶

C

calm　平靜

changing room　更衣室

compass　指南針

competition　比賽

colours　顏色

coral　珊瑚

crab　蟹

D

deckchair　躺椅

deep　深

different　不同的

dig　挖

dive　潛水

docked　停靠

dolphin　海豚

dorsal fin　背鰭

E

evening　黃昏

expert　專家

F

feel sick　生病

ferry　渡輪

fish　魚

fisherman　漁夫

fishermen
　　漁夫（fisherman的眾數）

fishing boat　漁船

fishing net　漁網

flip-flops　平底人字拖鞋

flippers　蛙鞋

float　浮

G

get dry　抹乾

get rid of　棄掉

H

harbour　碼頭

harbour office　碼頭辦事處

hull　船身

I

inflatable mattress　浮牀

investigate　調查

J

jellyfish　水母

L

life jacket　救生衣

lifeguard　救生員

life ring　救生圈

lighthouse　燈塔

line　繩子

M

map　地圖

marble　彈珠

mast　桅杆

meters　米

moulds　模子

motorboat　快艇

mystery　神秘事件

N

need　需要

night　晚上

O

oars　船槳

octopus

八爪魚（普：章魚）

out-of-date　過期

P

polluted　污染

port　碼頭

proud　驕傲

prow　船頭

R

reflection　倒影

replace　代替

rock　石頭

rotten　腐爛的

route　路線

rowing boat　手划船

rubber dinghy　橡皮艇

rubber ring　游泳圈

rudder　舵

S

sail　帆

sailing boat　帆船

sailor　船員

salmon　三文魚

salt　鹽

salty　鹹的

sand　沙

sandcastle　沙堡壘

sandals　涼鞋

sardine

沙甸魚（普：沙丁魚）

sea　海

sea anemone　海葵

seahorse　海馬

seashell　貝殼

seaside　海邊

sea urchin　海膽

seaweed　海草

shapes　形狀

shark　鯊魚

ship　郵輪

shivers　顫抖

shower　淋浴

smell　聞 / 氣味

snorkel　潛水換氣裝置

sole　比目魚

spade　鏟子

sponge　海綿

starfish　海星

steal　偷

stern　船尾

sun　太陽

sunglasses　太陽眼鏡

sunhat　太陽帽

sunbed　躺椅

sunset　日落

suntan lotion　防曬油

surrender　投降

surrounded　包圍

suspended　暫停

swimsuit

　　泳衣（普：游泳衣）

swordfish　劍魚

T

tentacles　觸手

today　今天

true　真的

tuna　吞拿魚

U

underwater　水中的

underwater mask　潛水面罩

W

water　水

waves　海浪

wind　風

看在一千塊莫澤雷勒乳酪的份上，你學得開心嗎？很開心，對不對？好極了！跟你一起跳舞唱歌我也很開心！我等着你下次繼續跟班哲文和潘朵拉一起玩一起學英語呀。現在要說再見了，當然是用英語說啦！

GERONIMO'S ISLAND
老鼠島地圖

往老鼠海峽

鯨魚出沒地

海盜貓船

海盜島

托圖加島

快樂島環礁

珊瑚礁

海豚灣

往鼠平洋

迷路貓港

角鯊
出沒地

貓牙灣

黑豹羣島

臭味港

往鼠西洋

壯鼠市

三鼠市

妙鼠城

鼠福巷

拔毛島

往老鼠海

老 鼠 島

Geronimo Stilton

EXERCISE BOOK
練習冊

想知道自己對 LET'S GO TO THE BEACH! 掌握了多少，
趕快打開後面的練習完成它吧！

ENGLISH!

7 LET'S GO TO THE BEACH! 到沙灘去！

ON THE BEACH 在沙灘上

⭐ 選出適當的英文詞彙,填在圖畫旁的橫線上。

> shower　　deckchair　　changing room
> sandals　　spade　　bucket　　rubber ring

1. _____

2. _____

3. _____

4. _____

5. _____

6. _____

7. _____

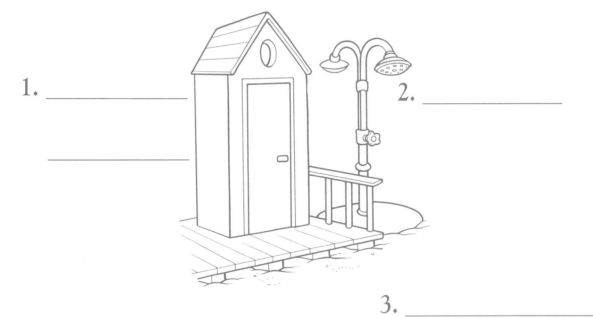

I HAVE GOT...　我有……

⭐ 看看下面的圖畫裏有些什麼，然後參照例子造句，在橫線上把句子補寫完整。

例：I have got a life ring.

1. You have got _____

2. She has got _____

3. He has got _____

4. We have got _____

5. They have got _____

LET'S DIVE IN! 一起去潛水！

⭐ 從下面的方框中選出適當的英文詞彙，填在每幅圖畫旁的橫線上。

1.

_____

2.

_____

3.

_____

> inflatable mattress
> rubber dinghy
> flippers
> underwater mask
> snorkel
> ship

4.

_____

5.

_____

6.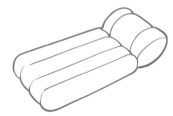

_____

LET'S GO SWIMMING!
一起去游泳！

⭐ 根據下面圖畫的意思，把每題中的詞彙重新排列，寫在橫線上，使它成為意思完整的句子。

1.

The | salty! | is | water | too

_____

_____

It's easier | in salt water, | to float | kids? | isn't it

2.

_____

_____

_____

3.

true! | That's

_____

_____

THE FISHING BOAT 漁船

⭐ 從下面選出適當的英文詞彙，填在每幅圖畫旁的橫線上。

life jacket　　binoculars　　sailor　　fisherman
map　　fishing net　　compass

1.

_____

2.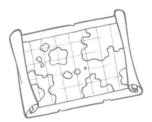

_____

3.

_____

4.

_____

5.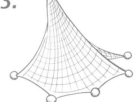

_____

6.

_____

7.

_____

WHAT HAVE THEY GOT?
他們有什麼？

⭐ 根據下面圖畫的意思和他們的話，完成句子。

I've got my map.

He has got _____ map.

I've got my binoculars.

She has got _____ binoculars.

I've got my red bucket.

I've got my yellow bucket.

Pandora has got _____ red bucket and Benjamin has got _____ yellow bucket.

I've got my compass.

He has got _____ compass.

6

ANIMALS LIVE UNDERWATER
住在水中的動物

⭐ 下面的動物都是住在水中的，你知道牠們的英文名稱嗎？試把下面的英文字母重新排列次序，在橫線上寫出來，然後給圖畫填上顏色。

1.

   h t s r f s i a

   _____

2.

   o r h s a s e e

   _____

3.

   l j l f y e h i s

   _____

4.

   r o c l a

   _____

5.

   t o o p u c s

   _____

ANSWERS 答案

TEST 小測驗

1. (a) beach umbrella (b) rubber ring (c) bucket (d) suntan lotion
   (e) starfish (f) seaweed (g) seahorse (h) jellyfish
2. (a) fish (b) fisherman / fishermen (c) fishing net (d) fishing boat
   (e) motorboat (f) port / harbour (g) sail (h) lighthouse
3. (a) I've got a blue bucket. (b) I've got a red bucket.
   (c) I've got a motorboat. (d) I've got an underwater mask.
4. (a) I haven't got an inflatable mattress. (b) I haven't got a beach towel.

   (c) I haven't got a boat. (d) I haven't got a sailing boat.

EXERCISE BOOK 練習冊

P.1
1. changing room 2. shower 3. deckchair 4. bucket
5. rubber ring 6. spade 7. sandals

P.2
Suggested answers:
1. You have got <u>a bucket.</u> 2. She has got <u>a pair of sandals.</u> 3. He has got <u>a rubber ring.</u>
4. We have got <u>two spades.</u> 5. They have got <u>two sunhats.</u>

P.3
1. underwater mask 2. ship 3. flippers 4. rubber dinghy
5. snorkel 6. inflatable mattress

P.4
1. The water is too salty! 2. It's easier to float in the salt water, isn't it kids?
3. That's true!

P.5
1. compass 2. map 3. binoculars 4. life jacket
5. fishing net 6. sailor 7. fisherman

P.6
1. his 2. her 3. her, his 4. his

P.7
1. starfish 2. seahorse 3. jellyfish 4. coral 5. octopus